ABCDE F.C.

CAL
APA
ЯAV

Dedicated to Jose Mourinho for ruining soccer forever.

You Go To War With the Roster You Have
A Soccering Book Told In Alphabet

Published by Never Knows Books

© 2018 P. Calavara, Never Knows Books, & ABCDE FC

ISBN: 978-1-946296-06-1

Never Knows Books is a subsidiary of the Never Knows Heavy Manufacturing Concern. The Calavara twins play extraordinary soccer in Olympia, WA. They score all the goals and nutmeg all the defenders and never ever give the ball away stupidly except sometimes. If you're interested in playing rec league Co-ed soccer in Thurston county, call SWSA and bug the hell out of the guy in charge. That jerk totally owes me money.

NEVER KNOWS BOOKS

For more soccer antics, check out **ABCDEfc.com**
For more P. Calavara hoolie business, check out **Calavara.com**
For all your heavy manufacturing concern needs, check out **NeverKnows.com**

You Go To War With The Roster You Have

A Soccering Book
Told In Alphabet
by P. Calavara

Armando always takes the blame
Each time we lose an Away game

Bernard knows what the fans all like
That's why he always tries a Bike

Cal's got two cultured left feet
And spends his pay on fancy Cleats

Dermot does a lot of whining
For a dude who's just a cheap Depth signing

Earl's sure that Extra Time
Is when he'll have his time to shine

Fynn's a gifted For-Mid-Fender

Which is why we put up with his benders

Gustav only loved two things
The first was Goals, the other flings

Harold's his own allegory
His **Howlers** tell his whole life story

Ignatz would be the perfect nine
If he wasn't Injured all the time

Jurgen keeps the channels clogged
Though he never runs, he only Jogs

Kristof's head is just a brick
What kind of **Keeper** only kicks?

Leonard stinks, but even so
We keep him on for his Long throws

Morton's first touch is a mess
So stick him in Mid and pray, I guess

Newt is tasked to mind the Net
Everywhere he looks, he sees a threat

Osmond's playing takes a toll
Often Offsides, plus some Own goals

Pascal goes out on a limb
Passing is for you, not him

Quentin used to be the Quickest
Nowadays he's just the thickest

Raul is only good at runs
Just boot it long, he'll play Route One

Sam Started til he missed a Sitter
Now he's a Sub and very bitter

Tufnell is sure that if he could
Get more Tattoos then he'd be good

Ulrich thinks that Ugly Wins
Should count as the 8th deadly sin

Valdo says some vapid stuff
Like, "near-Victory is near enough"

Will's a Winger to the end
He stays out wide and won't defend

Xapi must remember that
No one cares about his XG stat

Yoshi is an eager pup
But man those Yellows pile up

Zack's the Zonal Marking sort
Goes in too hard cuz he's too short

P. Calavara is an author and artist in Olympia, WA, where he shoots when he should pass and passes when he should shoot. He occasionally posts soccer jokes and comics at ABCDEfc.com.

The Gaffer thinks a 4-4-2
Is something only simps would do

CPSIA information can be obtained
at www.ICGtesting.com
Printed in the USA
LVHW07s0524010618
579207LV00009B/55/P